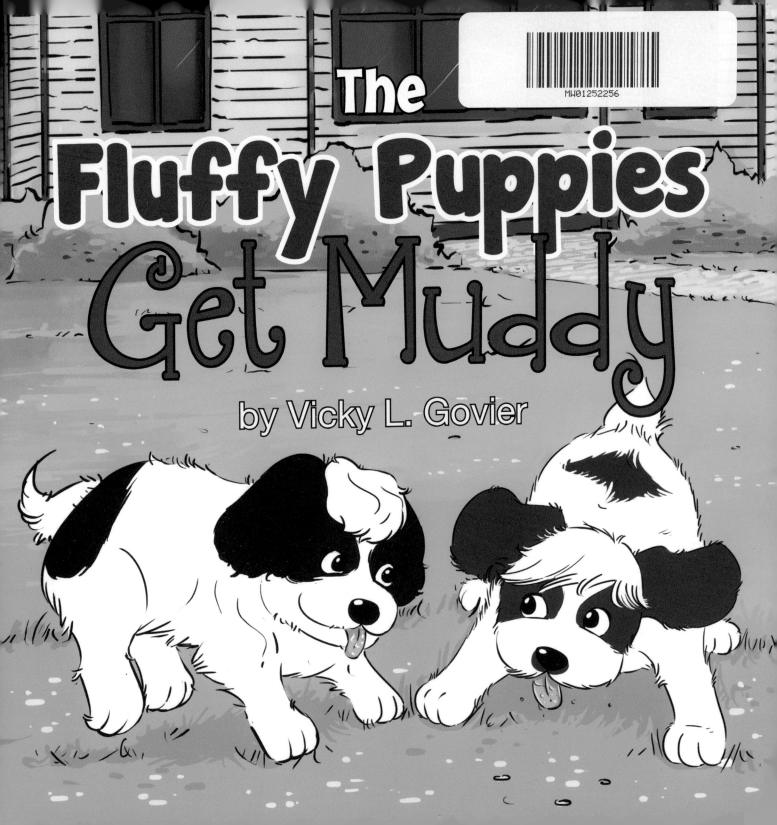

The Fluffy Puppies Get Muddy

by Vicky L. Govier

THE FLUFFY PUPPIES GET MUDDY
Copyright © 2014 by Vicky L. Govier

ISBN: 978-1-4866-0408-1

Word Alive Press
131 Cordite Road, Winnipeg, MB R3W 1S1
www.wordalivepress.ca

WORD ALIVE
—PRESS—

Library and Archives Canada Cataloguing in Publication

Govier, Vicky L., 1972-, author
    The fluffy puppies get muddy / Vicky L. Govier.

Issued in print and electronic formats.
ISBN 978-1-4866-0408-1 (pbk.).--ISBN 978-1-4866-0409-8 (pdf).--
ISBN 978-1-4866-0410-4 (html).--ISBN 978-1-4866-0411-1 (epub)

    I. Title.

PS8613.O974F48 2014   jC813'.6   C2013-908460-6
                                        C2013-908461-4

I dedicate this book to my husband, Rob, who is a constant support and encourager of pursuing my dreams.

This Book Belongs To

_____

Aaarff, Aaarfff,
Diesel and Ruby are two very fluffy puppies
that have come to live in a big house in a little
village with a sweet lady and her family.
One day the fluffy puppies were having a grand day
playing in the grass beside the big, big house.

They rolled...
They wiggled...
And they jumped...
But soon they got tired of playing in the same old spot.
They looked around to see where they could play next.

They looked at their owner planting pretty purple flowers in the garden, but she looked way too busy to play.

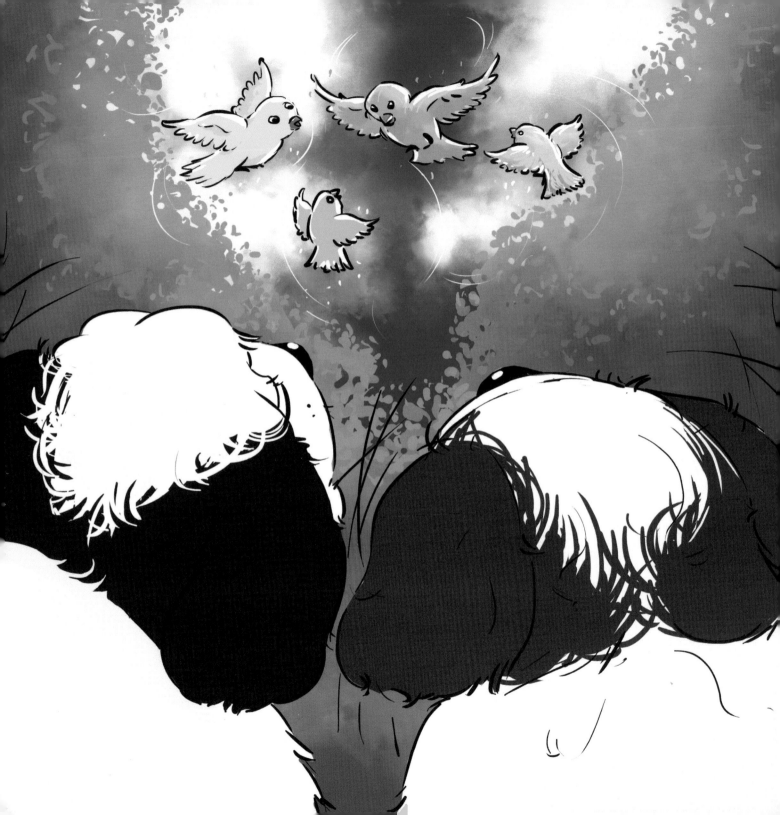

They looked at the birds swooping and chirping in the tree over their heads, but they were way too high to play.

They looked at the ground at a troop of little bitty ants all marching in a row, but they were way too small to play.

They looked at the road with cars whizzing by...
A big truck went past, and it let out a BIG
HooooONK!
The fluffy puppies jumped back.
Oh no, that was way too scary a place to play.

So with a quick look at each other and an *aaarf! aaarf!*
they bounded across the lawn in search of adventure.
Before long something caught their attention:
A soft *whooooosh* sound.
What could it be?
Being the curious type, the puppies ran to investigate!
Hmmmm...it looked like a long, black
snake stretched across the lawn.
They crept closer and discovered it had a hole in the end.
Diesel peered into the black hole.
Ruby gave it a sniff.

Suddenly, *whoooosh* came the sound again.
Water came streaming out!
It tickled their noses and swirled around their feet.
Oh wow, what fun, the water made a great big puddle!
Sooo...
They jumped in the puddle...
They wiggled in the puddle...
And they rolled in the puddle...

They were having a grand time.
Then they heard her,
their sweet, lovely owner calling their names.
"Diesel...Ruby...Where are you, my fluffy puppies?"
Happily they came running to see her.
Wet tails wagging and muddy ears flopping.
Uh oh...

Why was she looking at them that way?
Her mouth was open and her eyes were so wide!
They looked down at their dirty paws and dirty noses.
They looked back at their dirty tails and looked
up at their owner with sad, sorry eyes.
"You dirty little puppies!
What have you done? Your nice fluffy
fur is all full of icky sticky mud!
This is no good, no good at all! Off to the
bath you go, you not-so-fluffy puppies!"

Now, having a bath when you are a young
fluffy puppy is not a fun thing.
First came the water...
Then came the soap...
Then came even more water...
Over the back, under the tummy, around
the face, all while standing very still.

That is a very hard thing for a little fluffy puppy to do.
But, soon it was done and their sweet, lovely owner
wrapped them up snug in big, fluffy towels. She told
them she loved them and they knew it was true, even
when they got icky sticky and covered in mud.
So as they lay drying in the sun, the fluffy puppies
fell fast asleep. They dreamt a great dream of
whooshing and jumping and wiggling in mud!

The End!

About the Lake Amititlan Centre

One of my passions besides writing is a wonderfully special training centre in Lake Amititlan Guatemala.

I first visited the centre in 2011 and grew very interested in the vision and mission of the directors there.

This is an area with rampant crime, violence and very difficult situations. The main purpose of the centre is to provide pre-elementary education to the children in the surrounding community.

Preschool children receive the one-on-one attention from teachers they need and progress at a much faster rate than children in the public education system who have not received this head start.

The training center is also dedicated to serving those with special needs. Every year the center enrolls students who have added challenges and gives them equal opportunities for growth.

Ten percent of the proceeds from the sales of this book will go to help further the work at The Lake Amititlan Center. Thank you so much for supporting this school and its children so that they may have opportunities to thrive.

—*Vicky Govier*

For more information go to:

www.chglobal.org

CPSIA information can be obtained
at www.ICGtesting.com
Printed in the USA
408803LV00003B/5